Aunt Flossie's Hats
(and Crab Cakes Later)

Aunt Flossie's Hats
(and Crab Cakes Later)

by Elizabeth Fitzgerald Howard

Paintings by James Ransome

CLARION BOOKS

New York

On Sunday afternoons, Sarah and I
go to see Great-great-aunt Flossie.
Sarah and I love Aunt Flossie's house.
It is crowded full of stuff and things.
Books and pictures and lamps and pillows…

Plates and trays and old dried flowers…
And boxes
and boxes
and boxes
of HATS!

On Sunday afternoons when Sarah and I
go to see Aunt Flossie, she says,
"Come in, Susan. Come in, Sarah.
Have some tea. Have some cookies.
Later we can get some crab cakes!"

We sip our tea and eat our cookies,
and then Aunt Flossie lets us look
in her hatboxes.

We pick out hats and try them on.
Aunt Flossie says they are her memories,
and each hat has its story.

Hats, hats, hats, hats!
A stiff black one with bright red ribbons.
A soft brown one with silver buttons.
Thin floppy hats that hide our eyes.
Green or blue or pink or purple.
Some have fur and some have feathers.
Look! This hat is just one smooth soft rose,
but here's one with a trillion flowers!
Aunt Flossie has so many hats!

One Sunday afternoon, I picked out
a wooly winter hat, sort of green, maybe.
Aunt Flossie thought a minute.
Aunt Flossie almost always thinks a minute
before she starts a hat story.
Then she sniffed the wooly hat.
"Just a little smoky smell now," she said.
Sarah and I sniffed the hat, too.
"Smoky smell, Aunt Flossie?"

"The big fire," Aunt Flossie said.
"The big fire in Baltimore.
Everything smelled of smoke for miles around.
For days and days.
Big fire. Didn't come near our house
on Centre Street, but we could hear
fire engines racing down St. Paul.

Horses' hooves clattering.
Bells! Whistles!
Your great-grandma and I couldn't sleep.
We grabbed our coats and hats and ran outside.
Worried about Uncle Jimmy's grocery store,
worried about the terrapins and crabs.
Big fire in Baltimore."

Aunt Flossie closed her eyes.
I think she was seeing long ago.
I wondered about crab cakes.
Did they have crab cakes way back then?
Then Sarah sniffed Aunt Flossie's hat.
"No more smoky smell," she said.
But I thought I could smell some,
just a little.

Then Sarah tried a different hat.
Dark, dark blue, with a red feather.
"This one, Aunt Flossie! This one!"
Aunt Flossie closed her eyes and thought a minute.
"Oh my, yes, my, my. What an exciting day!"

We waited, Sarah and I.
"What happened, Aunt Flossie?" I asked.

"Big parade in Baltimore."

"Ooh! Parade!" said Sarah. "We love parades."

"I made that hat," Aunt Flossie said,
"to wear to watch that big parade.
Buglers bugling. Drummers drumming.

Flags flying everywhere. The boys—
soldiers, you know—back from France.
Marching up Charles Street. Proud.
Everyone cheering, everyone shouting!
The Great War was over!
The Great War was over!"

"Let's have a parade!" I said.
Sarah put on the dark blue hat.
I found a red one with a furry pompom.
We marched around Aunt Flossie's house.

"March with us, Aunt Flossie!" I called.
But she was closing her eyes.
She was seeing long ago.
"Maybe she's dreaming about crab cakes," Sarah said.

Then we looked in the very special box.
"Look, Aunt Flossie! Here's your special hat."
It was the big straw hat
with the pink and yellow flowers
and green velvet ribbon.
Aunt Flossie's favorite best Sunday hat!
It's our favorite story,
because we are in the story,
and we can help Aunt Flossie tell it!

Aunt Flossie smiled.
"One Sunday afternoon," she said,
"we were going out for crab cakes.
Sarah and Susan…"
"And Mommy and Daddy," I said.
"And Aunt Flossie," said Sarah.
Aunt Flossie nodded. "We were walking
by the water. And the wind came."

"Let me tell it," I said. "The wind came
and blew away your favorite best Sunday hat!"
"My favorite best Sunday hat," said Aunt Flossie.
"It landed in the water."
"It was funny," said Sarah.
"I didn't think so," said Aunt Flossie.

"And Daddy tried to reach it," I said,
"but he slid down in the mud. Daddy looked
really surprised, and everybody laughed."
"He couldn't rescue my favorite, favorite
best Sunday hat," said Aunt Flossie.

"And Mommy got a stick and leaned far out.
She almost fell in, but she couldn't reach
it either. The water rippled, and your
favorite best Sunday hat just floated by
like a boat!"

"Now comes the best part, and I'll tell it!"
said Sarah. "A big brown dog came.
It was walking with a boy.
'May we help you?' the boy asked.
'My dog Gretchen can get it.'
The boy threw a small, small stone.
It landed in Aunt Flossie's hat!
'Fetch, Gretchen, fetch!
Fetch, Gretchen, fetch!'

Gretchen jumped into the water
and she swam. She swam and she got it!
Gretchen got Aunt Flossie's hat!
'Hurray for Gretchen!'
We all jumped up and down.
'Hurray for Aunt Flossie's hat!'"

"It was very wet," said Aunt Flossie,
"but it dried just fine…almost like new.
My favorite, favorite best Sunday hat."

"I like that story," I said.
"So do I," said Sarah.
"And I like what happened next!
We went to get crab cakes!"

"Crab cakes!" said Aunt Flossie.
"What a wonderful idea! Sarah, Susan,
telephone your parents.
We'll go get some crab cakes right now!"

I think Sarah and I will always agree
about one thing: Nothing in the whole wide
world tastes as good as crab cakes.

But crab cakes taste best after stories…
stories about Aunt Flossie's hats!

To Lon (rock and sugar lump),
to Sarah and Jonathan (honey buns),
and in loving memory of Aunt Flossie
—E.F.H.

To my mother, Arsine,
thanks for all of your love and support
—J.R.

Clarion Books
a Houghton Mifflin Company imprint
215 Park Avenue South, New York, NY 10003
Text copyright © 1991, 2001 by Elizabeth Fitzgerald Howard
Illustrations copyright © 1991 by James Ransome

Oil paints on canvas were used to create the full-color art in this book.
The text was set in 14-point Galliard.

www.houghtonmifflinbooks.com

Printed in the U.S.A.

Library of Congress Cataloging-in-Publication Data

ISBN: 0-618-12038-6

Full cataloging information is available from the Library of Congress.

BVG 10 9 8 7 6 5 4 3 2 1

AFTERWORD

Aunt Flossie's Hats (and Crab Cakes Later) was published in 1991, ten years ago. And thanks to so many librarians, teachers, parents, and children, the book is still alive and well and reaching readers and listeners around the country. Thank you!

In Florida and Iowa, Texas and Hawaii, Michigan and Alabama, teachers and librarians let me know that they tell the story often and use the book for classroom activities: kids are making hats, tasting crab cakes, collecting family memoirs. "I love this story," people say. I am always so touched and humbled by these comments, and encouraged as well.

Perhaps it is true, as one reviewer noted, that the book conveys a universal reality that somehow tweaks a memory or touches off some spark of connection. Of course, James Ransome's vibrant paintings make the story fairly jump off the pages. (Thanks again, James!) And it turns out that almost everyone has, or has had, an Aunt Flossie or someone like her.

I'll tell you about mine.

Aunt Flossie with her "niece and godchild," Elizabeth Fitzgerald

Aunt Flossie was a real person, my real aunt and godmother. Sarah Florence James was born in 1888 into a close-knit middle-class black family. She was a granddaughter of Thomas J. Bradford, who held a respected position in a Maryland governor's household and a notable role at Bethel A.M.E. Church. Thomas Bradford had ten children, among them Sarah Elizabeth Bradford. Flossie was the eldest child of Sarah Elizabeth Bradford (Mama Sarah) and Richard Lewis James.

Mama Sarah was a seamstress; her husband worked at Hutzler's Department Store. He died suddenly in 1905, leaving her with three children, sixteen-year-old Sarah Florence (Flossie, also called Floss), eleven-year-old Lewis Bradford (Brad), and eight-year-old Bertha (Bert), my mother. Mama Sarah shared her house with her sister Mary (Aunt Mary), also a seamstress. They lived at 108 Centre Street, now part of the business district of Baltimore, around the corner from the grocery and provision store owned by their brother, James T. Bradford (Uncle Jimmy). I remember Aunt Flossie saying, "Uncle Jimmy's customers were rich white folks. He had crabs and terrapins and the best peaches anywhere."

Mama Sarah wanted her daughters to have a profession. They were to be teachers. Both Flossie and Bert graduated from the Colored High School and from the Colored Training School. (Up until the middle of the twentieth century, "colored" was the word used for African Americans and was generally applied to segregated facilities.) Flossie became an English teacher at the colored junior high school. She married Howard Wright, also a teacher, in 1923, and they moved into their house on McCulloh Street. Later, in 1928, Flossie got her B.S. degree from Morgan College.

Thomas J. Bradford. The original of this photograph is a tintype.

ABOVE: *Sarah Bradford James (Mama Sarah)*
CENTER: *Mary Bradford (Aunt Mary)*
BOTTOM: *James T. Bradford (Uncle Jimmy)*

Two years after Aunt Flossie and Uncle Howard were married, Aunt Mary moved in with them. And when Aunt Mary died, almost twenty years later, at the age of ninety-eight, her room became a storeroom—full of things to save, things to keep, like Thomas Bradford's Bible, where the family genealogy is written down.

Aunt Flossie is part of my earliest memories. Childless herself, she loved to show off my sister and me. When I was seven years old and Babs was four, we journeyed from Boston to Baltimore at Christmastime. Aunt Flossie figured out roles for us in her junior high school's Christmas program: costumed as angels, we proudly led the two lines as the whole student body entered the auditorium. We spent our childhood summers at Great-aunt Lulu's in Elkridge, near Baltimore; Aunt Flossie often had us come to her house in town, where we ate ice cream, tried on hats, and in the evenings sat on her white marble front steps playing guessing games. Sometimes she took us on Sunday outings. We went to the colored beach, or to a lovely country house where a lady provided wonderful chicken dinners for families and we children could run around the grounds or play on the swings. Aunt Flossie hired a driver for these expeditions; she didn't get a driver's license until later, when she was almost sixty.

Aunt Flossie talked often about the olden days. She told us about Uncle Jimmy the provision store owner grabbing her little sister, Bert, and threatening to carry her off to his butcher block and turn her into lamb chops. She told about her first birthday party, when she was five: "My mother made me a dress of pink China silk, and she spread a linen cloth under the dining room table so the little children wouldn't get ice cream on Uncle Jimmy's carpet." She told us about the great Baltimore fire of 1904 and about the thrilling parade when the colored soldiers returned from France after World War I.

Flossie as a young girl

After Great-aunt Lulu retired and moved to Boston, we no longer spent summers in Baltimore. Even so, when I graduated from high school, Aunt Flossie sent for me. She and Uncle Howard hosted a festive party, where she made sure I met all the "right" young people and their parents ("Here is Betty, my niece and my godchild"). In small and big ways she played a notable part in my college life: she sent a huge carton of A&P ginger cookies to be shared with my dorm mates, and she paid half my tuition. And later, always anticipating possible needs of her "niece and godchild," she appeared at the dock in Hoboken, New Jersey, as my still new husband, Larry, and I were boarding a student ship for Europe. She had brought a coat to lend me, which I declined (much to my regret later, as we shivered through Scotland). Through the years, she was always doing something thoughtful for me, and then for my children and my grandchildren.

Aunt Flossie never threw anything away. Her house was like a museum. She saved utility bills and Christmas and birthday cards and magazines. Sepia family photographs were stuffed into her bureau drawers along with pillow cases and tablecloths. Under her bed she stashed her shoes, all of them. "The old styles always come back," she would say firmly. The chaise longue in her bedroom was not for sitting; it was piled with linens, new, for

Flossie (second row, third from right) with her class at the Colored Training School

gifts or for future use. And there were layers of folded fabric cut in dress lengths ("You never know when you might need some black velvet or some summer cotton"). The clothes tree was fat with dresses, bathrobes, and coats. And, yes, there were boxes and boxes of hats, every single one indispensable.

"Could I have this navy blue one, Aunt Flossie?"

"Oh, no, my dear, I wear that one a lot."

In her nineties she was truly a presence. She was logical and down-to-earth but also quirky and quaint, with her patrician manner, her habits of thriftiness and her openhearted generosity, her surprising business daring (she quietly acquired some rental houses, including two on her street) and her safe deposit box stuffed with envelopes of money, her plastic grocery bag of bank books and keys and underwear and slippers, her superstitions and worries ("Don't sit on the cold stoop. You'll injure your internal organs."), her house ever more heaped up with books and trays and lamps and pillows and boxes and boxes and boxes of hats.

Bertha James (Bert), later Bertha James Fitzgerald

Aunt Flossie by herself was a story, and I wanted to write a book about her. But there were so many Aunt Flossie stories that I didn't know where to begin.

Then one day a little drama unfolded. The occasion was a family outing to the Inner Harbor for a crab dinner. . . .

My sister, Babs, and I arrived first. We chose a restaurant and sat on a bench enjoying the lovely parklike surroundings and watching for my husband and our parents and Aunt Flossie. Soon we saw them coming, stepping slowly along (everyone except Larry already a nonagenarian). But something was odd. Aunt Flossie, who always wore a noticeable hat, had no hat on her head . . . but there it was, secured between her thumb and forefinger: her favorite best Sunday hat. Dripping wet.

"What happened?" I asked Larry.

"Aunt Flossie's hat blew into the water, and we had quite a time rescuing it," he replied.

Trying to visualize the scene, I turned to my dad. "Paw, what did Aunt Flossie say when her hat blew away?"

With a bemused look he answered, "She said, 'I want my hat!'"

I want my hat! With those words, a picture book about Aunt Flossie started hopping around in my head. A summer afternoon. A family outing. Aunt Flossie in her Sunday hat. A breeze. Whoops . . . Aunt Flossie's hat . . . oh, no . . . it's in the water! It's drifting off . . . I want my hat! Help! Who can save Aunt Flossie's hat?

Lewis Bradford James (Uncle Brad)

The story turned out to have several layers of truth and fancy. I grounded it in the history to be found in the hats . . . my memories of how Babs and I had tried them on, and of the stories Aunt Flossie had told us. And memories of crab cakes, too—we went out to eat countless times with Aunt Flossie.

I never found out what really happened to Aunt Flossie's hat. That day the conversation moved on to other things. My father never told me, and my husband says he has forgotten. But a dog named Gretchen could have saved it, couldn't she?

The little girls in the story are the little girls who played at Aunt Flossie's house long ago. My sister, Babs, became Sarah, and I became Susan. I chose the name Sarah because it is a real family name. Aunt Flossie's first name was Sarah, as was her mother's, and Larry and I had just become grandparents of a new Sarah. So Sarah had to be in the book! I chose the name Susan to celebrate our daughter Sue. In addition, the name commemorates Maryland, where the black-eyed Susan is the state flower. Also, since I was feeling poetical, I liked having the second name begin with an *s*, for alliteration.

Uncle Howard died in 1945. Aunt Flossie retired from teaching in 1949. She stayed in the Baltimore row house where

LEFT: *Flossie as a young woman (date unknown)*

RIGHT: *Flossie and Howard on their honeymoon, Atlantic City, N.J., 1923*

she had been living since right after her honeymoon, enjoying social activities with her many friends, dispensing love and thoughtful gifts to her sister's family, steadfastly participating in church activities, occasionally traveling by bus to visit her "niece and godchild," and continuing to store up treasures on earth.

We celebrated Aunt Flossie's one hundredth birthday at St. James Episcopal Church in Baltimore on a sunny November day. She was wearing a brand-new red hat with a black veil. After the service there was a luncheon prepared by the guild members. Aunt Flossie sat happily surrounded by old and new friends, and called several of them over to meet "my niece and my godchild." Her health began to deteriorate shortly after that. She lived until within six weeks of her one hundred and first birthday. Sad to say, she never saw *Aunt Flossie's Hats (and Crab Cakes Later)*, which was published a year and a half after she died. I had read her the story, though, and she liked it. She would be amazed to know that people all over the United States know her name and know about her hats.

Aunt Flossie (right), Elizabeth Fitzgerald Howard (left), and a friend at Aunt Flossie's one hundredth birthday celebration

Once when an editor friend asked me, "Aren't there more stories about Aunt Flossie?" I mentioned the day Aunt Flossie told my husband and me about her grandfather Thomas Bradford's Bible. The Bible was in her house, in Aunt Mary's room—the locked bedroom at the end of the hall, so full of things to save, things to keep, that no one had been in there for decades—and Aunt Flossie had lost the key. "Tell the story of finding the Bible," suggested my friend, and I did some years later, in *What's in Aunt Mary's Room?* (Clarion, 1996).

What's so special about Aunt Flossie? Well, nothing, really. And yet, everything. Aunt Flossie's life was actually quite uneventful and ordinary, like that of any devoted family member, dedicated teacher, faithful churchgoer, and friend. But it is this very ordinariness that makes her real. When I talk about Aunt Flossie in workshops or in conference presentations, people are sure to come up and tell me how much Aunt Flossie reminds them of their own aunt or their grandmother or their Great-uncle Elmer, whose house they always went to on Saturdays and whose tools they played with. Or other family members.

Family stories are timeless, but once the storytellers are gone, the stories, too, can disappear. I greatly regret that I didn't ask Aunt Flossie to tell me more about growing up in Baltimore at the end of the nineteenth century and seeing the new century roll in when she was eleven. I especially wish I had heard the stories that Mama Sarah surely told her, about Grandpa Thomas Bradford, about the life of free blacks in Baltimore in the mid-1800s, just before the Civil War. Too bad. So much is lost that doesn't have to be. It is especially regrettable in the case of African American family stories. For most of our history very little of African American life appeared in print. We are dependent upon the oral tradition, which is often more reliable than the little that has been recorded. And before all the storytellers are gone, it is important that we try to find these stories and write them down, to preserve them as the vital part of American history and society that they are.

But everybody's family stories are valuable. As I stress to audiences whenever I can: Don't let the opportunity slip by. Talk to your grandparents, great-uncles, mothers, fathers. Ask your Uncle Elmer or Aunt Flossie to tell you stories. Write them down, or, maybe better, tape-record these special memories. Family stories connect us with our past and with our future.

They also connect us with other families. Sharing family stories—at an elementary school fair, a neighborhood picnic, an office get-together, a gathering of members of different church denominations—can build bridges as they reveal to us how much all of us have in common. We all share fundamental needs, hopes, values, and feelings. Whatever our ethnic, racial, or religious heritage, all our families have the same kinds of stories, because we all have our Aunt Flossies.

So let's celebrate more than the tenth anniversary of *Aunt Flossie's Hats (and Crab Cakes Later)*. Truly this occasion is most of all a chance to celebrate our collective treasury of stories, wonderful stories from all our families: Things to save. Things to keep. Things to share.